Ark Adventures

Noah and his wife think a flood
might be coming, so they have built
a big boat called the Ark. They are
sailing around the world to rescue the
animals before it starts to rain.

Let's all go on an animal adventure!

For Edward Bennett
S.G.

For James
A.P.

Reading Consultant: Prue Goodwin, Lecturer in literacy and children's books

ORCHARD BOOKS
338 Euston Road, London NW1 3BH
Orchard Books Australia
Level 17/207 Kent Street, Sydney, NSW 2000

First published in 2011
First paperback publication in 2012

ISBN 978 1 40830 558 4 (hardback)
ISBN 978 1 40830 566 9 (paperback)

A CIP catalogue record for this book is available from the British Library.

1 3 5 7 9 10 8 6 4 2 (hardback)
1 3 5 7 9 10 8 6 4 2 (paperback)

Printed in China

Orchard Books is a division of Hachette Children's Books,
an Hachette UK company.

Playful
Penguins!

Written by Sally Grindley

Illustrated by Alex Paterson

ORCHARD BOOKS

"Where are we, Mrs Noah?" asked
Noah one morning. "It's f-f-freezing.
All the animals are sh-sh-shivering.
I had to put the hamsters in with the
gorillas because they were so cold!"

"We're in the Antarctic," said
Mrs Noah. She was steering the Ark
through icy waters.

Noah picked up their *Big Book of Animals*.

"My hands are so c-c-cold. I can hardly turn the pages," he said. Then he squealed with excitement.

"Penguins! We'll find penguins here!"

6

"Don't they look smart?" said
Mrs Noah. "You'll have to dress up
to meet them."
"You're right! I'll go and change,"
said Noah.

Soon Noah came back. He was
wearing a black suit and carrying
a pair of flippers.

"You look very smart,
Mr Noah," said Mrs Noah.
"Just like a penguin!"

"Thank you, Mrs Noah," said Noah.
"Are you ready to go?" He lowered
the gangplank and fetched their
snowmobile.

They climbed aboard the snowmobile and drove onto the icy snow.

"Brrr! We'll have to find the penguins quickly or we'll f-f-freeze," said Mrs Noah.

Noah started the engine.

"Here we go!" he cried.

The snowmobile bumped and
bounced across the snow.
Noah and Mrs Noah bumped
and bounced in the snowmobile.
The snow seemed to go on
for ever.

They drove on and on.

"I hope we don't get lost," said
Mrs Noah.

"If I don't see a penguin soon I will
throw my flippers out of the
snowmobile," grumbled Noah.

Suddenly, something black whizzed past them across the ice.

"What was that?" cried Noah.

Another black thing whizzed past,
going the other way.

"Penguins!" cried Mrs Noah.

"They're penguins."

Noah stopped the snowmobile and jumped off. But the ice was very slippery. He fell flat on his bottom.

When he tried to stand up, he just fell over again!

The two penguins slid past him.
"Try sliding on your tummy like
them," laughed Mrs Noah.

"No, thank you," said Noah. He grabbed his flippers from the snowmobile and put them on. "Now I can stand up," he said. "Wait for me, penguins!"

"Whooaa!"
Noah slipped across
the ice . . .

"Whoops!"
Noah slid across the ice . . .

"Wheee!"

Noah slithered across the ice . . .

"It's not easy being a penguin!"

he cried.

Just then, something pink and fluffy whizzed past him. "What was that?" said Noah.

"It's me!" laughed
Mrs Noah, getting up.

"Look what I've got!"

She held two fish up in the air.

The penguins waddled happily

towards her.

"Come with us," Mrs Noah said.
"We've got lots of fish and you don't
have to go in the cold water to
catch it."

The penguins dropped onto their
tummies and began to follow
Mrs Noah.
"Come on, Noah," she called. "Let's
get back to our nice warm Ark."

Noah tried to walk after them, but fell flat on his bottom again. "I've had enough of this," he grumbled.

He turned over onto his tummy.

"That's the way to do it," laughed

Mrs Noah.

When they reached the snowmobile,
they helped the penguins on board.
Noah scrambled in and started
the engine.

"Off we go," he cried.

"Hold on tight."

They whizzed off across

the ice.

At last they saw the Ark ahead of them. "I can't wait to toast my toes," said Noah.

"You mean your flippers!" laughed

Mrs Noah.

SALLY GRINDLEY · ALEX PATERSON

All priced at £8.99

Orchard Books are available from all good bookshops, or can be
ordered from our website: www.orchardbooks.co.uk,
or telephone 01235 827702, or fax 01235 827703.

JUST ME AND MY MOM

BY
MERCER MAYER

*For my new son Benjamin
and his Momma*

A Random House PICTUREBACK® Book

Random House 🏠 **New York**

We went to the city,
just me and my mom.
Mom gave me some money
to buy tickets for the train.

I wanted to help Mom get on the train
but the steps were too high.
So Mom helped me instead.

But when the conductor came by,
the tickets were gone.
So Mom paid the conductor
some more money.

The city was very busy.
I held Mom's hand so she
wouldn't be scared.

We went to the Museum
of Natural History.
They had rooms full of
old dinosaur bones.

I picked up a little dinosaur egg
to show to my mom.
But someone ran up and grabbed it.
I wasn't going to hurt it.

I tried on some costumes,
just for Mom.
But the museum guard
didn't like that.

Then we went next door
to the Aquarium.

There were lots of fish
in a big tank of water.

They had some seals doing a show.
Mom got mad because
she couldn't find me.
I ran up front to get
a closer look at the seals.

We went to the art museum,
but it only had a lot of weird pictures
and I was getting tired.

After that, we went to a very
nice restaurant for lunch.
We didn't stay, though.

We decided to have a hot dog from
a stand. That was more fun anyway.

Mom wanted to go to a big store
full of dresses and stuff like that. Yuck.

Mom even made me try on some clothes.
She bought me a new suit.
Some guy measured me and stuck pins all over
my clothes.

We passed by the toys.
I found the stuffed animal
I always wanted
but Mom said, "It's time to go."

We took a taxi to the train station.
I got to ride in the front seat.
The taxi driver drove real fast.
That was cool.

I let Mom buy the tickets this time.
She said she didn't have
enough money to buy more tickets
if these got lost.
"Good idea, Mom!"

We had fun, just me and my mom.
I even stayed awake
all the way home — well, almost.